TOM'S MAGNIFICENT MACHINES

LINDA SARAH

BEN MANTLE

To Mum and Dad, with love - LS

For Mia Wreford-Bush - BM

SIMON & SCHUSTER
First published in Great Britain in 2018 by Simon & Schuster UK Ltd
1st Floor, 222 Gray's Inn Road, London, WC1X 8HB • A CBS Company • Text copyright
© 2018 Linda Sarah • Illustrations copyright © 2018 Ben Mantle • The right of Linda
Sarah and Ben Mantle to be identified as the author and illustrator of this work has
been asserted by them in accordance with the Copyright, Designs and Patents Act,
1988 • All rights reserved, including the right of reproduction in whole or in part in
any form • A CIP catalogue record for this book is available from the British Library
upon request.
978-1-4711-2245-3 (HB) • 978-1-4711-8394-2 (PB) • 978-1-4711-2247-7 (eBook)
Printed in China • 10 9 8 7 6 5 4 3 2 1

TOM'S MAGNIFICENT MACHINES

LINDA SARAH

BEN MANTLE

SIMON & SCHUSTER

London   New York   Sydney   Toronto   New Delhi

Tom and his dad loved making things together, especially things that moved.

It had started simple.
Go-karts and skateboard-chariots pulled with string.

But then their inventions got bigger, faster, crazier.
Now their home was full of whirring, humming, hovering creations.

And giggles.

Lots and LOTS of giggles.
Life was as sweet as spring.

But then, a change, quick as lightning. Dad lost his job. And it felt like Tom had lost his funny, smiling dad,

fellow inventor of magnificent machines.

The ones they'd already made became rusty and dusty
– old, forgotten friends.

Sadness clouded the house like a winter sky.

And then, even worse, the next day news.
They would have to leave.

"I'm so sorry, Tom, we just can't afford to live
in this house any more."

Tom could not, WOULD not leave.

"NO!" he shouted.

But Tom's angry words floated over Dad's head,
away, away, like soundless bubbles.

So Tom had to do something.
He went out on his triple-extender trolley-bike,

thinking, thinking, thinking . . .

. . . then, quick as that leaf falling, he had an idea.

It was BIGGER than autumn
– a brilliant, hope-filled, **HUGE** idea!

He rushed home to share it with Dad.

But Dad just murmured,

"Hmmm, that's nice."

So Tom tried again.

And again.

"You see?! We can open our house to visitors so everyone can see our amazing inventions. We can call it

The Museum of Vehicles Made From Things Not Usually Used For Making Vehicles!"

"You know what," said Dad, after what felt like hours.
"That's not a bad idea, Tom!"

And he smiled for the first time in eleven sunsets.
That month, their home buzzed, busy with excitement.

Together Tom and Dad
tested and fixed,

scrubbed, oiled and painted

and polished until their vehicles
glittered blink-bright.

Nothing, nothing like this
had ever been seen,

or even IMAGINED!

Visitors came from near and far. They gaped at the miniature banana-powered rocket.

They gasped at the ingenious Mappolator.

They gawped at the piano airship.

They stared at the tandem bathicoptor,

the mechanical hummingbird.

the remote-control submarine,

All around the museum were sighs of wonder and laughter like sunlight.

They giggled at the moustachicoplor zig-zagging wonkily.
They chuckled at the high-powered, self-flushing, superspeed-system toilet racer.

Visitors poured in from near and even more far
and, after a few weeks . . .

. . . Dad announced they could stay in their house.

Their home.

But then one cold night, a whirlwind skittled through the dark, sucking up all things and spitting them far.

Their home was now mostly rubble,
just a few strewn bits of broken exhibits
poking skywards in the white snowfields.

Why can't good things ever stay the way they are? thought Tom.

"We can rebuild it!" said Dad brightly, full of badly-hidden sad.

But Tom said, "It could happen again.
The weather is as unpredictable as dreams."
Tom couldn't stand it.

Why, why, **WHY**?!

He tried riding and thinking again,
but his head felt as empty as that sky.

But when he arrived home,
Dad was grinning wildly.
He'd had a really, really BIG idea.
"We'll rebuild our home into an amazing,

MOVING museum!"

"Dad," said Tom proudly, grinning wider than summer, "you're a genius. A complete GENIUS!"

That month they oiled, painted, polished, fixed, scrubbed and cleaned.

And soon their mobile museum-home could

walk

float

gallop

and even . . .

FLY!

And each evening, after museum closing time,
Tom and his dad would surf the skies,

whooping-happy and racing shooting stars.